Handyman Doug

First published in 2008 by
Franklin Watts
338 Euston Road
London
NW1 3BH

Franklin Watts Australia
Level 17/207 Kent Street
Sydney
NSW 2000

A CIP catalogue record for this book is available
from the British Library.

ISBN 978 0 7496 7979 8 (hbk)
ISBN 978 0 7496 7987 3 (pbk)

Series Editor: Jackie Hamley
Series Advisor: Dr Barrie Wade
Series Designer: Peter Scoulding

Printed in China

Franklin Watts is a division of
Hachette Children's Books,
an Hachette Livre UK company.

Handyman Doug

by Mick Gowar

Illustrated by Peter Cottrill

W
FRANKLIN WATTS
LONDON•SYDNEY

On Monday, Doug drove his van down Delia Drive and …

... crash!

"Look what you've done
to my car!" shouted
Mr Brown.

"Don't worry," said Doug,
"I'll come back tomorrow
and fix it."

On Tuesday, Doug mended the car.

"Nearly finished," said Doug. "Oops …"

"Look what you've done
to my window!" yelled
Mr Brown.

"Don't worry," said Doug,
"I'll come back tomorrow
with some glass."

On Wednesday, Doug
put in the new window.

"Finished!" said Doug.

"Look what you've done to our house!" cried Mr and Mrs Brown.

"Oops," said Doug,
"I'll come back tomorrow
with some paint."

On Thursday, Doug painted the house ...

19

… and the garden
and the washing.

"Look what you've done to my best dress!" sobbed Mrs Brown.

"Don't worry," said Doug. "I'll come back tomorrow with a hose and bucket."

On Friday, Doug washed the garden, the washing and splashed Mr and Mrs Brown.

"Oops," said Doug.
"Goodbye!" said Mr
and Mrs Brown.

On Saturday and Sunday, Doug went fishing ...

... and shopping.

On Monday, Doug drove his van down Delia Drive and …

... crash!

"Don't worry, Doug!"
said Mr Brown.
"The garage will fix it!"

Leapfrog has been specially designed to fit the requirements of the National Literacy Framework. It offers real books for beginning readers by top authors and illustrators. There are 26 Leapfrog stories to choose from:

The Bossy Cockerel
ISBN 978 0 7496 3828 3

Bill's Baggy Trousers
ISBN 978 0 7496 3829 0

Little Joe's Big Race
ISBN 978 0 7496 3832 0

The Little Star
ISBN 978 0 7496 3833 7

The Cheeky Monkey
ISBN 978 0 7496 3830 6

Selfish Sophie
ISBN 978 0 7496 4385 0

Recycled!
ISBN 978 0 7496 4388 1

Felix on the Move
ISBN 978 0 7496 4387 4

Pippa and Poppa
ISBN 978 0 7496 4386 7

Jack's Party
ISBN 978 0 7496 4389 8

The Best Snowman
ISBN 978 0 7496 4390 4

Mary and the Fairy
ISBN 978 0 7496 4633 2

The Crying Princess
ISBN 978 0 7496 4632 5

Jasper and Jess
ISBN 978 0 7496 4081 1

The Lazy Scarecrow
ISBN 978 0 7496 4082 8

The Naughty Puppy
ISBN 978 0 7496 4383 6

Big Bad Blob
ISBN 978 0 7496 7092 4*
ISBN 978 0 7496 7796 1

Cara's Breakfast
ISBN 978 0 7496 7093 1*
ISBN 978 0 7496 7797 8

Why Not?
ISBN 978 0 7496 7094 8*
ISBN 978 0 7496 7798 5

Croc's Tooth
ISBN 978 0 7496 7095 5*
ISBN 978 0 7496 7799 2

The Magic Word
ISBN 978 0 7496 7096 2*
ISBN 978 0 7496 7800 5

Tim's Tent
ISBN 978 0 7496 7097 9*
ISBN 978 0 7496 7801 2

Sticky Vickie
ISBN 978 0 7496 7978 1*
ISBN 978 0 7496 7986 6

Handyman Doug
ISBN 978 0 7496 7979 8*
ISBN 978 0 7496 7987 3

Billy and the Wizard
ISBN 978 0 7496 7977 4*
ISBN 978 0 7496 7985 9

Sam's Spots
ISBN 978 0 7496 7976 7*
ISBN 978 0 7496 7984 2

Look out for Leapfrog

FAIRY TALES

Cinderella
ISBN 978 0 7496 4228 0

The Three Little Pigs
ISBN 978 0 7496 4227 3

Jack and the Beanstalk
ISBN 978 0 7496 4229 7

The Three Billy Goats Gruff
ISBN 978 0 7496 4226 6

Goldilocks and the Three Bears
ISBN 978 0 7496 4225 9

Little Red Riding Hood
ISBN 978 0 7496 4224 2

Rapunzel
ISBN 978 0 7496 6159 5

Snow White
ISBN 978 0 7496 6161 8

The Emperor's New Clothes
ISBN 978 0 7496 6163 2

The Pied Piper of Hamelin
ISBN 978 0 7496 6164 9

Hansel and Gretel
ISBN 978 0 7496 6162 5

The Sleeping Beauty
ISBN 978 0 7496 6160 1

Rumpelstiltskin
ISBN 978 0 7496 6165 6

The Ugly Duckling
ISBN 978 0 7496 6166 3

Puss in Boots
ISBN 978 0 7496 6167 0

The Frog Prince
ISBN 978 0 7496 6168 7

The Princess and the Pea
ISBN 978 0 7496 6169 4

Dick Whittington
ISBN 978 0 7496 6170 0

The Elves and the Shoemaker
ISBN 978 0 7496 6581 4

The Little Match Girl
ISBN 978 0 7496 6582 1

The Little Mermaid
ISBN 978 0 7496 6583 8

The Little Red Hen
ISBN 978 0 7496 6585 2

The Nightingale
ISBN 978 0 7496 6586 9

Thumbelina
ISBN 978 0 7496 6587 6

Rhyming stories are available with Leapfrog Rhyme Time.

* hardback